GIRLS' HEALTH™

POLYCYSTIC OVARY SYNDROME

FRANCES E. RUFFIN

rosen publishing's
rosen central®

NEW YORK

To my cousin, Dr. Virginia Wright

Published in 2012 by The Rosen Publishing Group, Inc.
29 East 21st Street, New York, NY 10010

First Edition

Library of Congress Cataloging-in-Publication Data

Ruffin, Frances E.
Polycystic ovary syndrome/Frances E. Ruffin.
p. cm.—(Girls' health)
Includes bibliographical references and index.
ISBN 978-1-4488-4576-7 (library binding)
1. Polycystic ovary syndrome—Juvenile literature. I. Title.
RG480.S7R84 2012
618.1'1—dc22

2010044138

Manufactured in the United States of America

CPSIA Compliance Information: Batch #S11YA: For further information, contact Rosen Publishing, New York, New York, at 1-800-237-9932.

CONTENTS

INTRODUCTION

As a young girl enters puberty, her body undergoes many changes that signal she is becoming an adult. She grows taller, her breasts begin to develop, hair grows under her arms and in her pubic area, and she begins to menstruate. Typically, these changes occur in every adolescent as she develops into a young woman. But for some girls, certain bodily changes are not typical. They may be embarrassing and even give the girls who have them reason to worry about their health. These signs are brought on by a common hormonal disorder called polycystic ovary syndrome (PCOS). The changes these teens experience are due to hormonal imbalances. According to the U.S. Department of Health and Human Services, this disorder affects more than five million teen girls and women of childbearing age. PCOS often begins after a girl has her first period, and she may notice that she has some of the following symptoms:

- Acne, oily skin, or dandruff that is difficult to treat
- Dark patches of skin on her neck, under her breasts, armpits and/or thighs
- Sudden weight gain, especially around the waist
- Excessive hair growth (called hirsutism) on her face, breasts, hands, and feet
- Male-patterned baldness, causing hair loss at the hairline and the top of the head
- Pelvic pain

Polycystic ovary syndrome affects one in ten women in the United States. Women with this disorder can lead healthy lives by being well-informed about PCOS, seeking medical treatment, and changing their lifestyle.

Girls who have PCOS may have these symptoms of the condition throughout their lives. The symptoms can become even more complicated and challenging to their health at menopause, the time when a woman no longer has monthly periods. Who gets PCOS? Many medical researchers believe that your genes, what you inherit from your family, may play a role in the condition. If your mother, or another close female relative, has PCOS, you may have up to a 40 percent chance of developing it, too.

Currently, there is no known single factor that causes polycystic ovary syndrome. Doctors believe that the symptoms are caused by imbalances in certain hormones, such as estrogen, progesterone, and testosterone, in a woman's body. Although genetics (heredity) likely influences whether or not a woman will have PCOS, certain factors such as environment, lifestyle, and emotional stress may trigger its onset.

CHAPTER one

WHAT IS PCOS?

Having PCOS means that there is an imbalance in certain hormones in your brain and in your ovaries. Hormones are natural chemicals produced by certain glands that travel through your bloodstream to specific organs. They act as messengers and "inform" specific organs how they must function. For example, two groups of these messengers, estrogens and androgens, are sex hormones. They are responsible for how the reproductive organs in humans grow and develop.

The female sex hormones estrogen and progesterone are produced primarily in the ovaries, whereas the androgen testosterone is mainly produced in the male testes. It is normal for girls to have some androgens in their bodies and for boys to have some estrogen, but the amounts differ greatly for each sex. Both groups of sex hormones really get to work during puberty. Puberty is the period of life when humans first become able to reproduce sexually. The genitals, or sex organs, begin to mature. Girls, at about the age of ten, and boys, at about the age of twelve, experience growth spurts, pubic hair, and body odor, among other changes in the body. Both sexes are on their way to maturing into women and men.

As people mature, sex hormones help them develop secondary sex characteristics. Boys grow facial hair, and their voices deepen because they have higher levels of testosterone. Girls can credit estrogen for helping them develop larger breasts and wider hips.

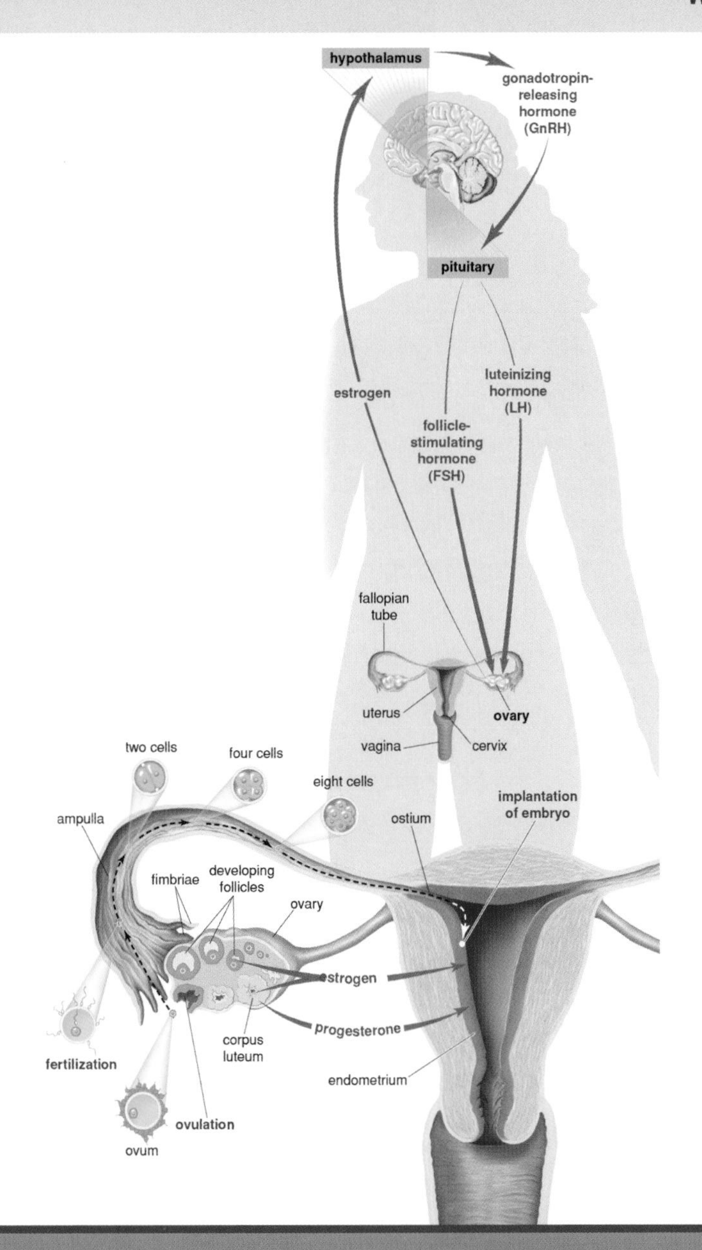

The hypothalamic-pituitary-ovarian axis is made up of the hypothalamus at the base of the brain, the pituitary gland just below it, and the ovaries, one on each side of the pelvis. The stages of the menstrual cycle are controlled by the interaction of hormones that are released by these organs. The bottom picture depicts the development of an ovum, or egg.

Another group of hormones fulfills an important role in regulating a girl's menstrual cycle. This process begins in the hypothalamus, a collection of cells in the center of the brain, and then goes to the pituitary, a pea-sized gland at the base of the brain. The hypothalamus and the pituitary regulate the body's normal processes, such as sleeping, eating, blood pressure, and body temperature. For women, the hypothalamus and pituitary also regulate the function of the ovaries, such as preparing the body for pregnancy and having monthly periods. At the beginning of your menstrual cycle each month, the hypothalamus releases a chemical called gonadotropin-releasing hormone (GnRH) that signals the pituitary to release two hormones: luteinizing hormone (LH) and follicle-stimulating hormone (FSH). Acting as messengers, LH and FSH stimulate the ovaries to produce estrogen and progesterone. Other hormones made in the ovaries also "feed back" to the hypothalamus and pituitary when estrogen and progesterone levels are sufficient to reduce the production of GnRH, FSH, and LH. All these messengers work together throughout the monthly menstrual cycle to create a careful balance of necessary hormones.

OVULATION

The ovaries, two organs about the size and shape of an almond and located on either side of your pelvis, store tiny eggs in sacs called follicles or cysts. The ovaries of a girl in her early teens may contain as many as a half million eggs. During the menstrual cycle each month, a chain of hormonal events prepares the uterus for an egg (sometimes more than one) to become fertilized. (The uterus is a pear-shaped organ in the lower abdomen of a girl that can hold and nurture an unborn baby.) This process begins with a surge of LH and FSH hormones sent from the pituitary to the ovaries, where an ovum, or egg, begins to mature. When these hormones reach the ovaries, they cause the sac, or cyst, around the maturing egg to produce estrogen. This higher level of estrogen also prompts

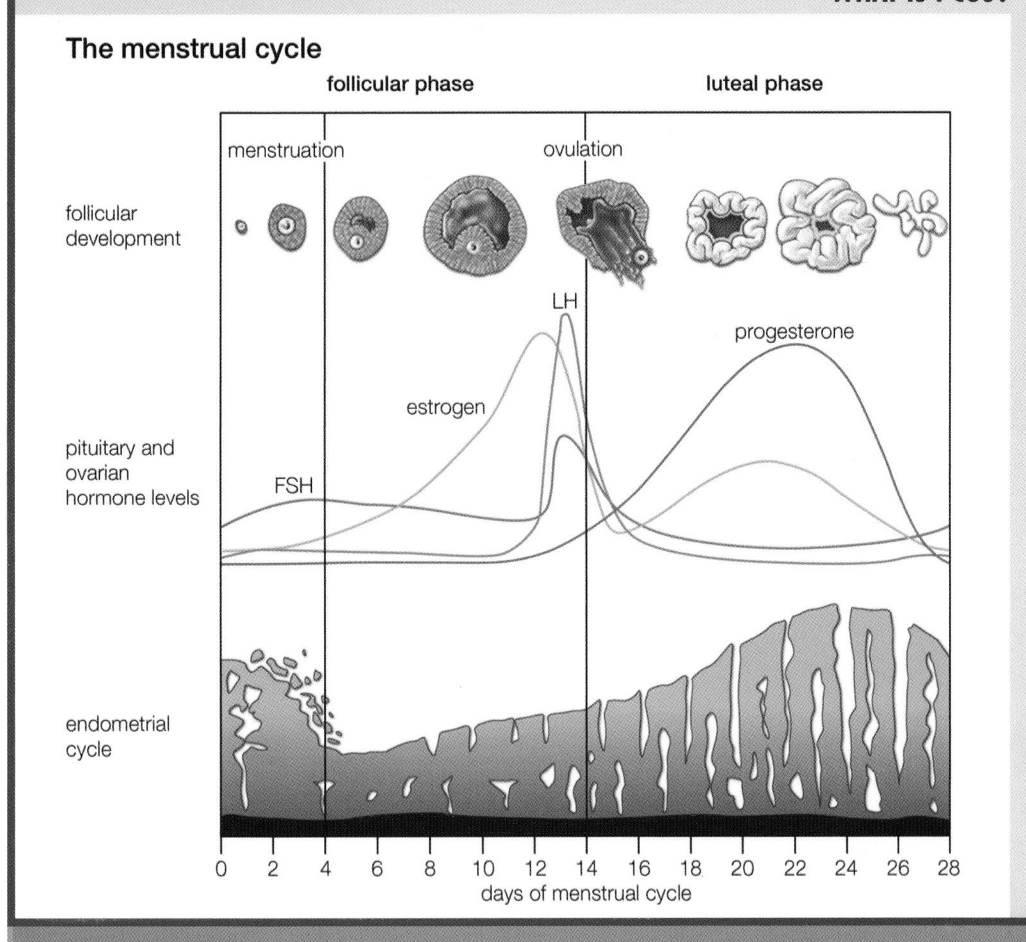

This graph shows the changes in a follicle's development, hormone levels, and the lining of the uterus (endometrial cycle) during a normal monthly menstrual cycle.

the uterus to create a thick, cushiony lining of the endometrium (the layer of tissue that lines the uterus) into which a fertilized egg can implant.

Generally, fourteen days after a girl's last menstruation, the mature egg splits from its sac and is released from the ovary to begin a journey down one of the two fallopian tubes to the uterus. This event is called ovulation. The empty ovarian sac, which is called the corpus luteum, produces both estrogen and progesterone. These hormones cause the lining of the uterus to thicken even further. At the same time, up in the brain, the pituitary receives the message to shut down its production of LH.

MENSTRUATION

If a woman has intercourse while the egg is in the uterus or in transit to the uterus, and her partner's sperm fertilizes the egg, she may become pregnant. If she does not become pregnant, the egg dissolves. The lining of her uterus is shed and passes out of her body as menstrual blood. After the bleeding ends, the cycle starts again. For most girls and women, the menstrual cycle is a twenty-eight-day pattern of hormones that interact with one another. It can take about two years for a girl's cycle to become regular and for her to have a period each month. What happens if periods don't become regular or if they stop?

SYMPTOMS OF PCOS

Irregular periods or missing periods in a girl older than sixteen is often the first medical sign that she may have PCOS. Here's how hormonal imbalance plays a major role in this irregularity. Girls who have PCOS maintain higher-than-normal levels of LH. For the new menstrual cycle to begin, their bodies must have low levels of LH at the end of the cycle. This scarcity of hormones stimulates the hypothalamus to signal the pituitary. The message: release a large surge of FSH so that a new cycle can begin. Without this surge, the egg for that cycle fails to mature, and ovulation will not begin. The egg remains as a cyst, and a girl with this condition will not menstruate. This failure to ovulate is called anovulation. (A woman might not ovulate because of a hormonal imbalance.) Women who are consistently anovulatory frequently have long, irregular menstrual cycles, and they may not have a period for months or years. The most common cause of chronic, or consistent, anovulation is PCOS. Over time, when

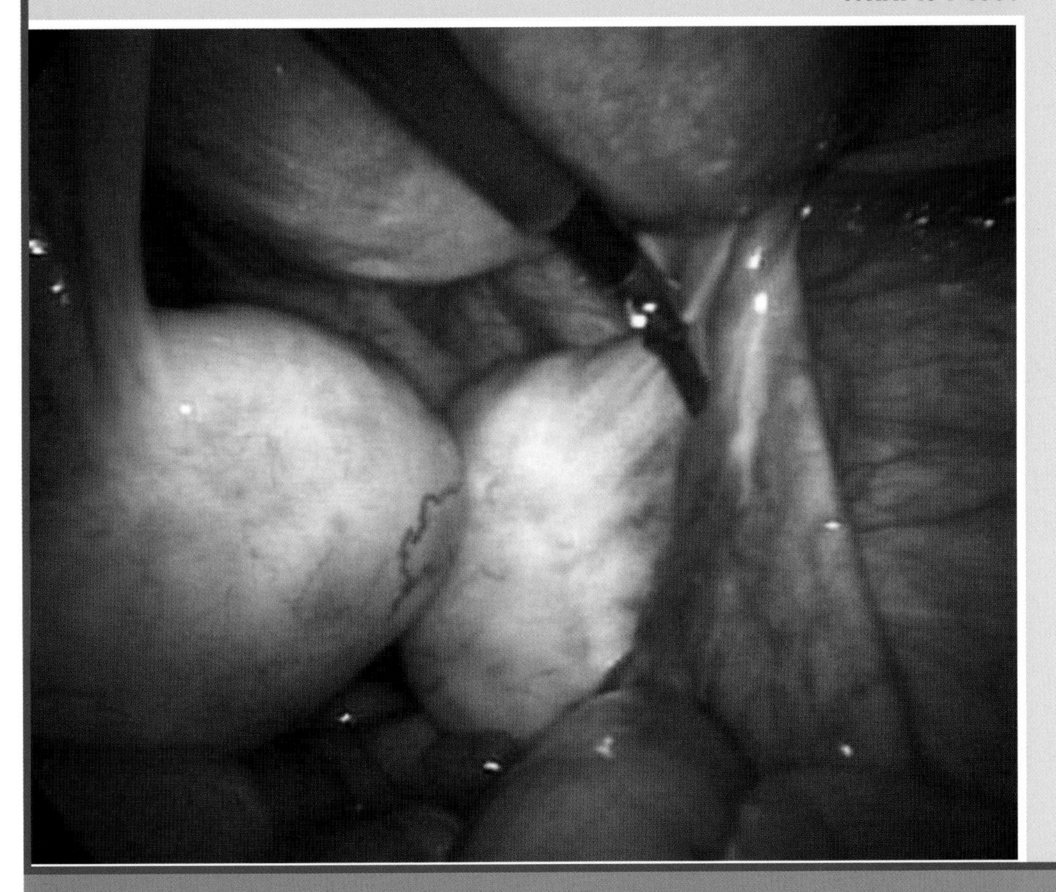

An endoscope, a device with a light and a camera, reveals a woman's uterus *(top)* and polycystic ovaries *(white)* that are filled with cysts.

menstruation is irregular or stops completely, the ovaries of many women will contain numerous small, undeveloped cysts of eggs that have never matured. The ovaries of some women who do not have PCOS, however, may also have cysts. The suppression or unusual absence of menstrual periods is known as amenorrhea. Hormone imbalance caused by PCOS affects a young woman's entire body. She may experience a collection of symptoms that, over time, can become disorders that create long-term health problems.

The higher levels of LH brought on by PCOS not only change a girl's menstrual cycle, but also make her body produce higher levels of androgens than normal. These male hormones stimulate the pancreas, a gland in the abdomen that produces the hormone insulin. Insulin plays many vital roles, such as regulating how the cells in the body grow. Among other functions, insulin enables the body to metabolize, converting into energy the foods—carbohydrates (sugars and starches), lipids (fats), and proteins—that people eat.

For some people, including women who have PCOS, the cells in the body become resistant to the positive effects of insulin. When this happens, the cells demand even higher levels of the hormone, creating a condition known as insulin resistance. When a woman's body becomes resistant to insulin, she is at risk for a host of health problems, most of which require medical care. The most serious conditions brought on by insulin resistance include type 2 diabetes, high cholesterol, high blood pressure, and even endometrial cancer. Several of these conditions can cause heart disease. Symptoms of these health problems usually occur over many years. Some women may not even know they have PCOS until they find that they have difficulty conceiving. PCOS is the most common cause of infertility in women.

MYTHS AND FACTS

MYTH **Women who have PCOS are infertile and therefore can never become pregnant.**

FACT PCOS is a major cause of infertility, but not all women who have this disorder are infertile. There are also various treatments for women with PCOS who have difficulty conceiving.

MYTH **Missing your period for three months is a sure sign of having PCOS.**

FACT It can take up to two years after her first period for a girl's menstrual cycle to become regular. If she has other signs of PCOS, such as obesity, hair loss, and/or acne, she should consider seeing her doctor.

MYTH **PCOS can be cured.**

FACT At this time, there is no cure for this disorder, only treatments. Medical scientists are currently working to understand the causes of PCOS and find a cure.

CHAPTER two

DIAGNOSING PCOS

How is PCOS diagnosed? The symptoms of this disorder may make a girl seek help from doctors specializing in different areas of medicine. She may be embarrassed by a bad case of acne or the dark hairs that keep growing over her upper lip, so she may visit a dermatologist. A girl might make an appointment to see her family doctor because she has suddenly put on a lot of weight and can't lose it. Many young women who suffer from missed periods or from amenorrhea visit or will be referred to a gynecologist. This is a doctor who cares for women's sexual and reproductive health and treats disorders that affect the female reproductive organs. These problems can range from menstrual cycle issues to tumors. Because gynecologists also diagnose and treat the symptoms of PCOS, they are familiar with the signs and health problems that come with this condition. Some gynecologists specialize in treating only children and teens. These doctors are called pediatric gynecologists.

Women who show symptoms of PCOS may be referred to an endocrinologist. This is a specialist who diagnoses the diseases of the endocrine system and its hormones. These diseases and conditions include diabetes, obesity, infertility, and thyroid diseases. A pediatric endocrinologist is a specialist who treats not only these conditions, but also physical growth and sexual development disorders in young people.

WHEN TO SEE A GYNECOLOGIST

Whether a girl is in the best of health or has some medical issues that need to be treated, the American Congress of Obstetricians and Gynecologists recommends that she make her first visit to a gynecologist between the ages of thirteen and fifteen. When you make your appointment with a

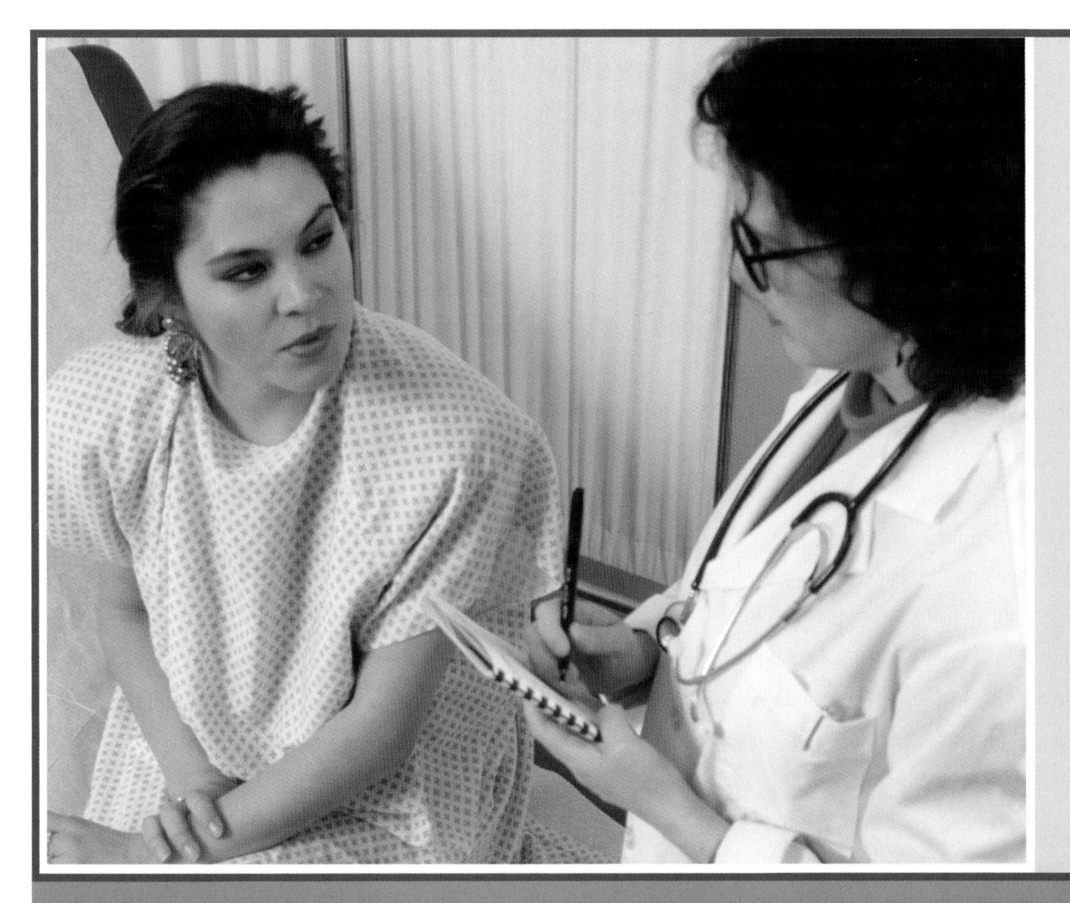

As a young woman matures, she becomes more responsible for her health. This role includes visiting a doctor when she has concerns about unfamiliar or troublesome health symptoms.

gynecologist, ask your mother or another adult woman you feel comfortable with about what to expect during your visit.

There is no single test that can diagnose polycystic ovary syndrome, but there are several steps that will help your doctor detect this condition. Based on the symptoms that a girl describes, a physical examination and a series of lab tests will be used to make—or rule out—a diagnosis of PCOS. Experts who study the disorder affirm that the first step in diagnosing PCOS is to rule out other conditions that cause similar symptoms.

Be prepared to provide your doctor with information about your medical history. While waiting in the office to see the doctor, you will be asked to complete a form with questions that include listing all the illnesses you may have had, the names of any medicines you are taking, if you have had surgery, whether you drink or smoke, if you have ever been pregnant, and the date of your last period.

THE PHYSICAL EXAM

The next step is the physical examination. The doctor will listen to your heart and lungs and take your pulse and blood pressure. He or she may measure your weight and height to determine your body mass index (BMI). This is a calculation that measures body fat based on a person's height and weight and determines if a person is underweight or overweight.

Your doctor will also check for the "cosmetic" or physical signs that are characteristic of PCOS and affect your appearance, such as acne, oily skin, dandruff, skin discolorations, abnormal hair growth or loss, and small skin tags in the armpits or on the neck. Your doctor may inquire about your sleep habits to determine if you have sleep apnea. Sleep apnea is a worrisome condition where a person stops breathing for short periods, sometimes causing him or her to wake up and gasp for air. It can sometimes be associated with PCOS.

A pelvic ultrasound exam is another step toward diagnosing PCOS. This painless test is performed while you lie on an examining table and

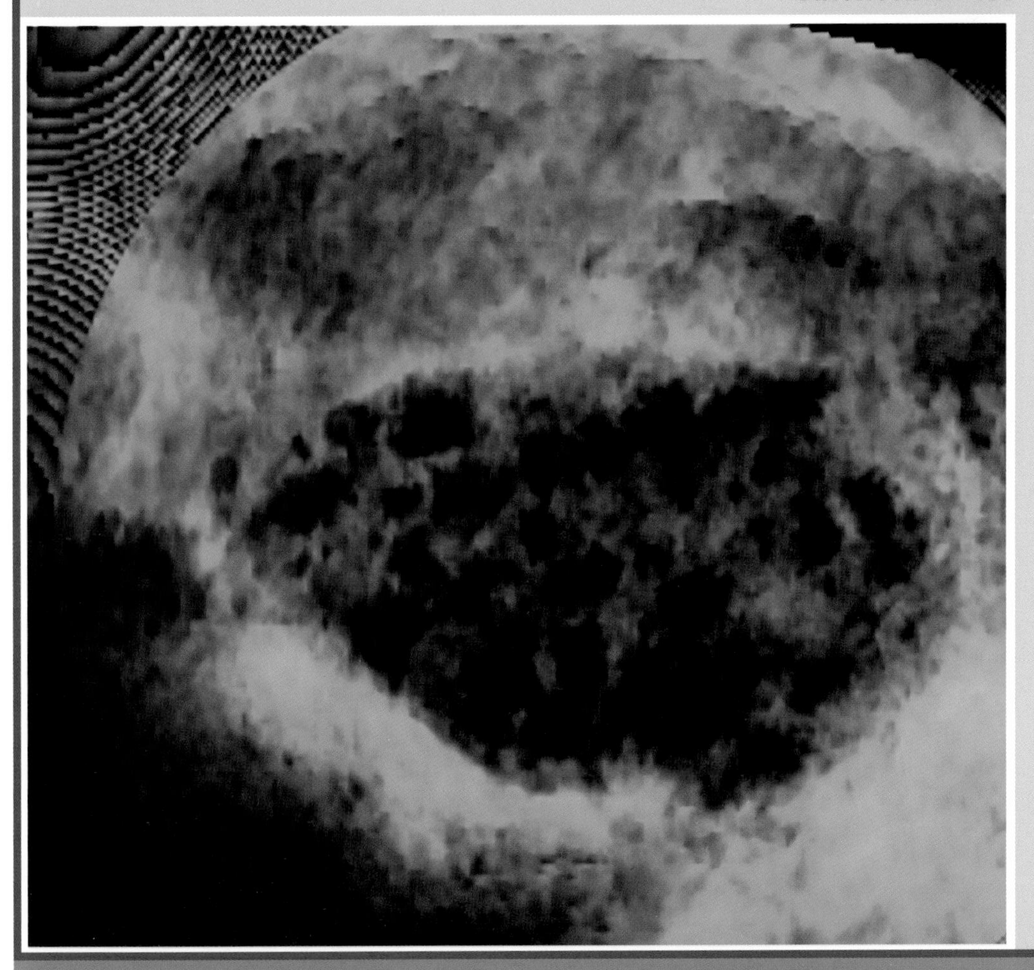

A doctor may order a pelvic ultrasound scan to help diagnose PCOS. In the ultrasound image shown here, an ovary is filled with abnormal cysts (black dots) that formed when follicles failed to ovulate.

the doctor, or a technician, moves a wandlike device over your lower abdomen. The wand sends sound waves to a computer, which makes a picture on a screen. Your doctor will be able to view your ovaries and uterus. The images on the screen can show if your ovaries are enlarged or swollen with small cysts. (It is important to note, though, that women who don't have PCOS may have ovaries with many cysts.) If you have had many irregular periods or

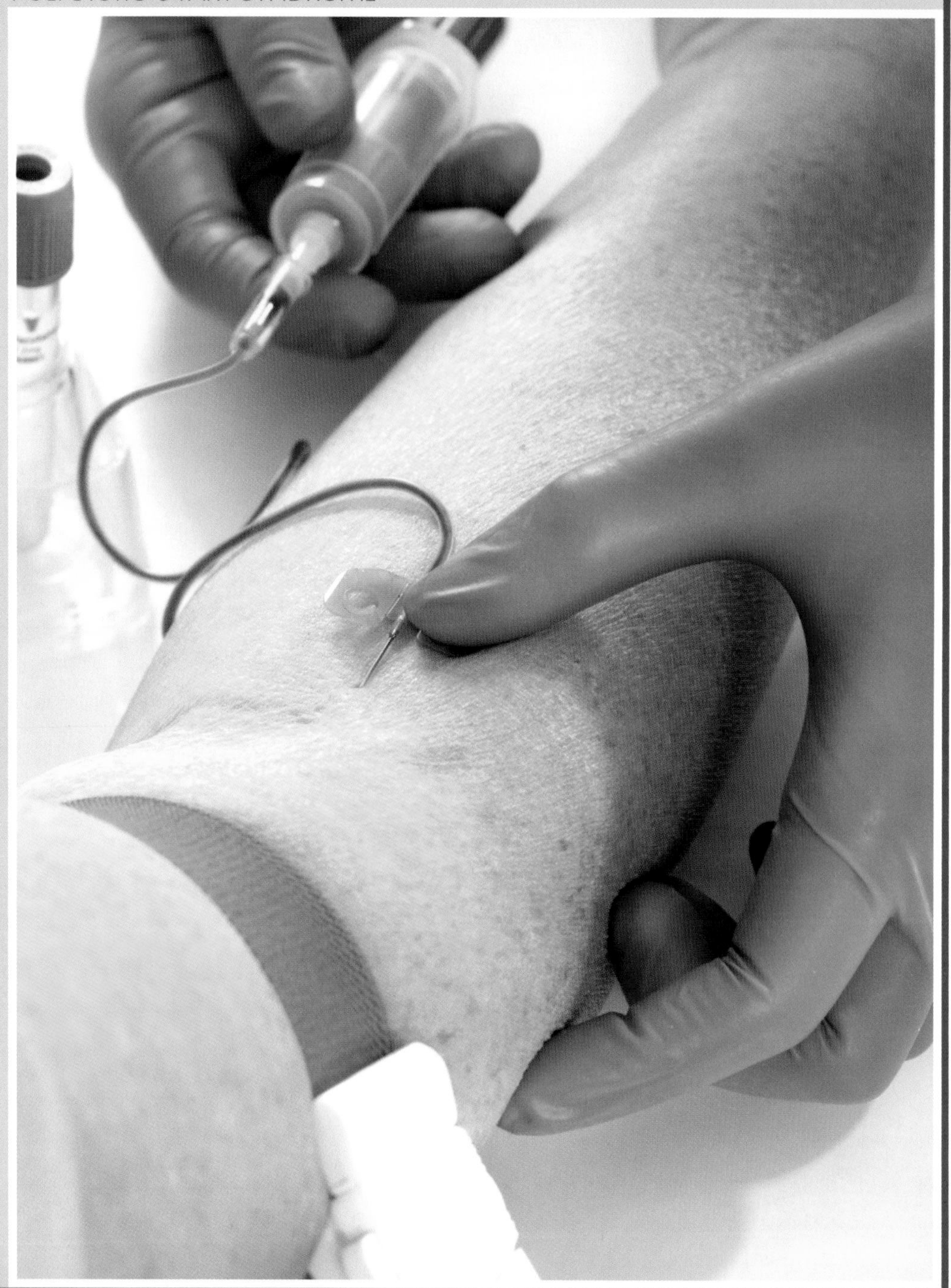

Blood tests are important tools for helping diagnose PCOS and other health conditions caused by the disorder.

do not menstruate, an ultrasound image might show that the lining in your uterus is thicker than normal.

CHECKING YOUR BLOOD SUGAR

Blood tests can provide important information about your body and how it is functioning. The results of certain blood tests can be the final step toward providing a diagnosis for PCOS. One blood sample that your doctor will send to a lab for testing is the oral glucose tolerance test (OGTT), which shows if a person has abnormal levels of blood glucose (sugar).

The doctor may also order blood tests to check for elevated levels of the male hormone testosterone. Medical research has shown that abnormal blood levels of insulin also stimulate the ovaries to produce too much testosterone. This causes a woman to develop acne, grow excessive facial hair, or lose hair on her scalp.

The OGTT is used to help determine whether a person is at risk for or has type 2 diabetes, a serious disease that is often called adult-onset diabetes. It measures how your body uses glucose. Simple and complex sugars (carbohydrates) are in foods such as bread, cereal, pasta, rice, fruits and vegetables, and sweets. Your body converts carbohydrates into glucose to use as a main source of energy. The glucose that is not used is stored in your liver and muscles for future use. Glucose can stay longer, though, in the blood of people whose bodies are resistant to insulin.

For the OGTT, blood is drawn from a person who has fasted (that is, not had anything to eat or drink for eight to twelve hours—drinking water is permitted). After blood is drawn, the person is given a very sweet glucose preparation to drink. Two hours later, another blood sample is drawn. Normal fasting blood levels are less than 100 mg/dL (milligrams per deciliter is the traditional unit for measuring blood glucose). A person with blood glucose levels that read 100 to 125 mg/dL are considered to be prediabetic or have insulin resistance.

INSULIN RESISTANCE

People who are insulin resistant—a common disorder of women with PCOS—are at risk of developing type 2 diabetes. In fact, the U.S. Department of Health and Human Services reports that in recent studies, more than 50 to 60 percent of women with PCOS are at risk of diabetes or will develop diabetes before the age of forty. Over time, serious diseases from this condition can threaten a person's health and even her life. It can damage your kidneys, cause heart disease and blindness, and destroy tissue, which can cause a person to lose a limb by amputation. So it is essential that people be evaluated for their risk of developing diabetes and work with a doctor who can provide early intervention to prevent and treat it.

Other blood tests will check a woman's blood lipids (fats), including cholesterol, and triglyceride levels, since abnormally high levels of them are associated with PCOS.

10 GREAT QUESTIONS TO ASK YOUR DOCTOR

1. I'm worried that I might have PCOS. What are the most common symptoms?
2. What tests will my doctor perform to diagnose PCOS?
3. Could the pain in my pelvic area on the lower right side of my abdomen have anything to do with PCOS?
4. I have PCOS, and I haven't menstruated in seven months. How can my doctor help me have regular periods?
5. How many days are there between period to period in a normal menstrual cycle?
6. I am taking a contraceptive pill to make my periods regular. Is there any risk?
7. I've been told that PCOS can cause some really serious diseases. What are they?
8. I have PCOS, and my doctor told me to lose weight. I'm not that much overweight, so why is this important?
9. I am losing hair on my head, but little hairs are popping out on my chin, over my lip, and in lots of other places. What can I do?
10. Is there a cure for PCOS?

CHAPTER three

HOW IS PCOS TREATED?

If you are diagnosed with PCOS, your doctor will likely inform you that, so far, it has no cure. You may feel that this is unfair, especially if you are suffering from some really unpleasant symptoms from the disorder. However, there are many ways to manage PCOS. Medical science now has many treatments available that can help relieve symptoms and lessen your risk of developing serious illness.

Most doctors prescribe oral contraceptive pills, also known as birth control pills, or the pill, to help regulate the menstrual cycle. It can also help with other signs of the disorder, such as facial hair growth, hair loss, and acne. The main purpose of the pill is to prevent pregnancy, but these medications are also very effective at regulating unbalanced hormones. In addition, contraceptive medication comes in forms besides pills, such as patches, shots, and rings placed inside the vagina. In general, there are two types of contraceptive pills. One type is a combination of estrogen and progesterone, while the other contains only progesterone.

How do contraceptive pills work to regulate the menstrual cycle of someone with PCOS? A girl who experiences a normal menstrual cycle will ovulate. During the cycle, estrogen and progesterone cause the endometrium, the lining of the uterus, to thicken. This is to prepare for a mature egg. At the end of the ovulation process, her progesterone levels increase and then drop off sharply. This signals the lining of the uterus to shed. Girls with PCOS do not ovulate

Doctors prescribe birth control pills to treat the hormonal imbalance that causes PCOS in many teens and women.

regularly. The lining of the uterus does not shed regularly. Eventually, the lining becomes so thick that it sloughs off and can cause heavy menstrual-type bleeding. To prevent this, contraceptive pills supply the progesterone that will enable the uterine lining to shed.

PRESCRIBING ORAL CONTRACEPTIVES

Some people may be concerned about the risks of taking an oral contraceptive. When you are prescribed any medicine, you should always discuss its potential risks, as well as the benefits, with your doctor. It's really important that your doctor has your complete medical information. Do you have a history of blood clots or migraine headaches? Does anyone in your family have a history of blood clots or strokes? Do you smoke? Do you take other medications, such as certain antibiotics or herbal supplements, on a regular basis? Your doctor will take your answers into consideration before prescribing the pill.

Most women under the age of thirty-five who take the pill and who do not smoke will have few or no health problems. According to the Center for Young Women's Health, a division of Adolescent and Young Adult Medicine in the Department of Gynecology at Children's Hospital in Boston, Massachusetts, if you have any of the following symptoms while taking oral contraceptive pills, call your doctor right away:

- Abdominal or stomach pain (severe)
- Chest pain (severe), cough, shortness of breath
- Headache (severe), dizziness, weakness, or numbness
- Eye problems (vision loss or blurring), speech problems
- Severe leg (calf or thigh) pain

It is also important to remember to follow your doctor's instructions while taking the pill. There are many brands of contraceptive pills, so you should know how long the cycle is for each set of pills and what time of day is best for taking your type of pill. Be sure to take other precautions if you are sexually active. The pill will not protect you from sexually transmitted diseases (STDs), so you should always also use condoms if you are sexually active. Health professionals advise young people that abstinence is the best protection against pregnancy or STDs.

PREVENTING DIABETES

The drug metformin, also known by the brand name Glucophage, can successfully control elevated blood sugar levels for people with PCOS. It is a medicine taken by mouth twice a day to treat prediabetes and type 2 diabetes. However, it was also discovered to be useful in treating some of the unwanted signs of PCOS. Most young women who have PCOS have elevated levels of insulin, which cause patches of thick, dark, and discolored skin at the back of the neck, under the arms, and on the skin of the lower abdomen. High blood levels of insulin can stimulate the ovaries to produce higher-than-normal levels of androgen (male) hormones. This can cause a girl to grow hair where she doesn't want it to grow—on her upper lip and other parts of her body—or she may lose hair from her scalp. Metformin can reduce the effects of these conditions. It produces few side effects for most of those who take it, but some people experience stomach upset. Doctors can suggest a lower dose for a patient for a few days to build up to the prescribed dose.

Spironolactone, also known by the brand name Aldactone, is another medicine that can deal with more than one symptom of PCOS while lessening the discomfort and health risks. Spironoactone is a diuretic, or water pill, often used to reduce swelling in people who have high blood pressure. Bonus effects are that it reduces facial hair growth and helps clear up PCOS-related acne.

More than 70 percent of girls and women with PCOS have hirsutism, or excessive hair growth, and severe acne. To treat these conditions, doctors may prescribe antiandrogens, medications that decrease the

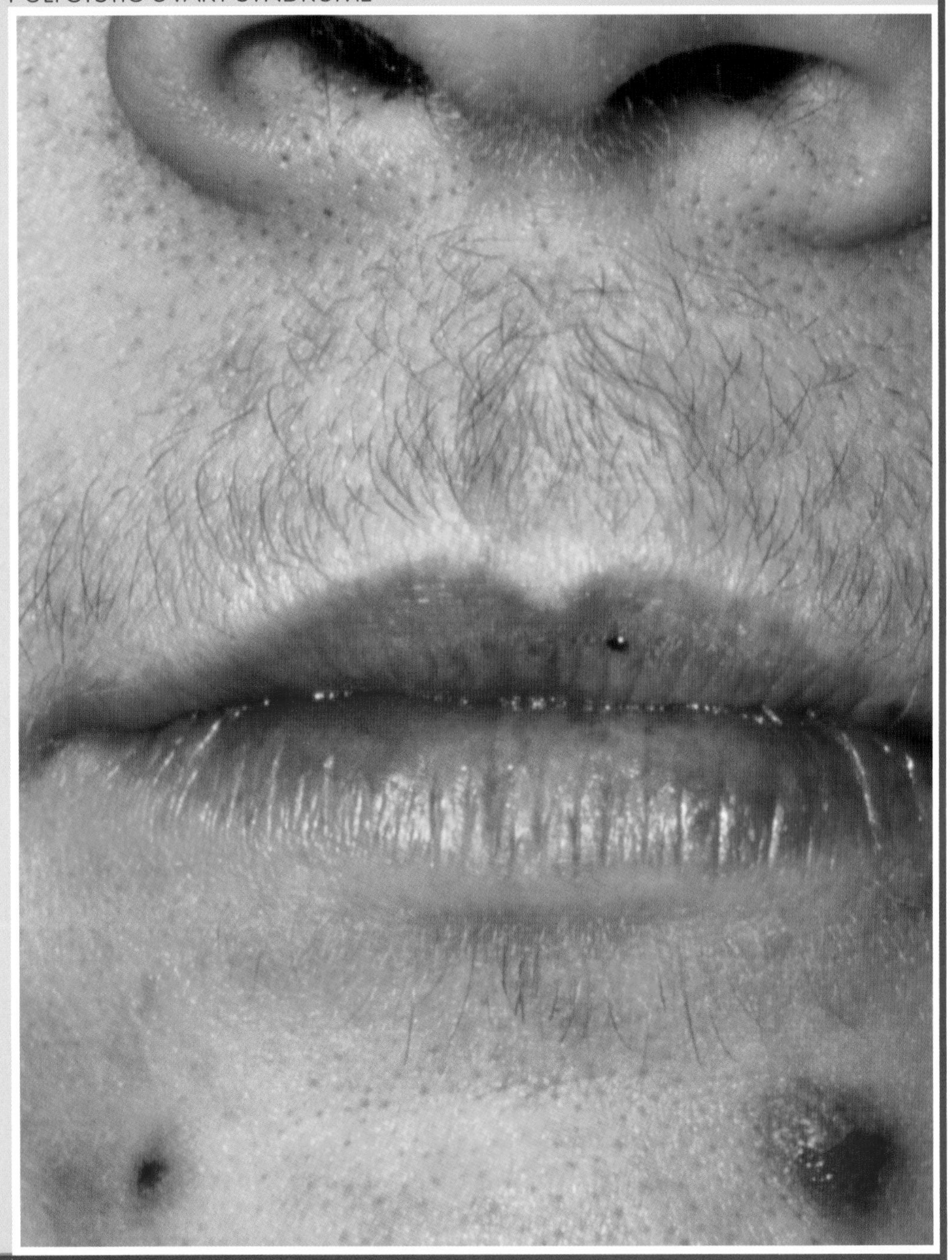

Some of the most unpleasant symptoms of PCOS for the women who have the disorder are acne and the growth of excess facial hair (hirsutism). Both conditions can be treated with medications.

body's ability to make androgens. By lowering the levels of androgens, they reduce the hirsutism and acne that are often caused by too much testosterone. One such antiandrogen drug is eflornithine, also known as Vaniqa.

INFERTILITY AND PCOS

PCOS is a major cause of infertility in women. Not all infertility is caused by PCOS, though. A woman who has difficulty getting pregnant may undergo many tests to determine if she is infertile and if her infertility is related to PCOS. To treat PCOS-associated infertility, doctors may prescribe clomiphene, a medication that induces ovulation, and metformin, which combats insulin resistance. This combination has enabled many women with PCOS to conceive.

PCOS AND METABOLIC SYNDROME

Metabolic syndrome is a condition that causes many of the same symptoms and serious health problems associated with PCOS. Although women with polycystic ovary syndrome are at greater risk of developing metabolic syndrome, other women and men suffer from this disorder, too. According to the American Heart Association, in a 1999–2002 survey, 9.4 percent of adolescents in the United States, from ages twelve to nineteen and representing about 2.9 million young people, suffer from metabolic syndrome.

Metabolic syndrome is a condition in which the body's metabolism has gone awry. People with this condition, which is also called syndrome X, have three or more symptoms of an impaired metabolism, including the following:

- Obesity, usually with increased weight/fat in the waist
- High blood pressure

Perhaps one of the most dangerous symptoms caused by PCOS is obesity. When a girl or woman carries too much body fat, she is at risk of developing several health-threatening illnesses.

- Elevated levels of triglycerides, blood fats, and low levels of the good cholesterol, HDL
- Insulin resistance

In fact, the primary cause of metabolic syndrome is insulin resistance. Like PCOS, this syndrome has no cure, but it is generally brought on when people are overweight or obese. Metabolic syndrome is also linked to other health-damaging diseases, such as diabetes, breast cancer, and colon cancer. Symptoms and even the start of serious diseases can be delayed or prevented. Medical experts urge people to change habits from those that damage their health (poor diet, smoking, and lack of exercise, to name just a few) and adopt a healthy lifestyle. In fact, a commitment to a healthy lifestyle can reverse some of the symptoms and health problems in both PCOS and metabolic syndrome.

CHAPTER four

YOUR HEALTH TEAM

If you are one of the one in ten girls and women in the United States who has been diagnosed with PCOS, you can be sidelined by this disorder, especially if you have symptoms that make you feel sick or unattractive. But you can, after a bit of time, accept the diagnosis and make the decision to not be overwhelmed by PCOS. You can take charge of your health.

LEARN ABOUT PCOS AND WHO CAN HELP

First, try to learn as much as you can about the disorder and its symptoms and what it can do to your body and your health. Next, create a support team of people to confide in. Team members might include your mother, an older sister, another adult woman you are at ease with, and a best friend or two. These team members can give you a lot of emotional support, so be upfront about what you need from them. Let them know, too, that at times you may not be the most cheerful girl in town, but you will always appreciate having them be there for you.

Your team should also include your doctors and other medical professionals who are involved in your treatment. It may be helpful to join a PCOS support group in your area to learn from the

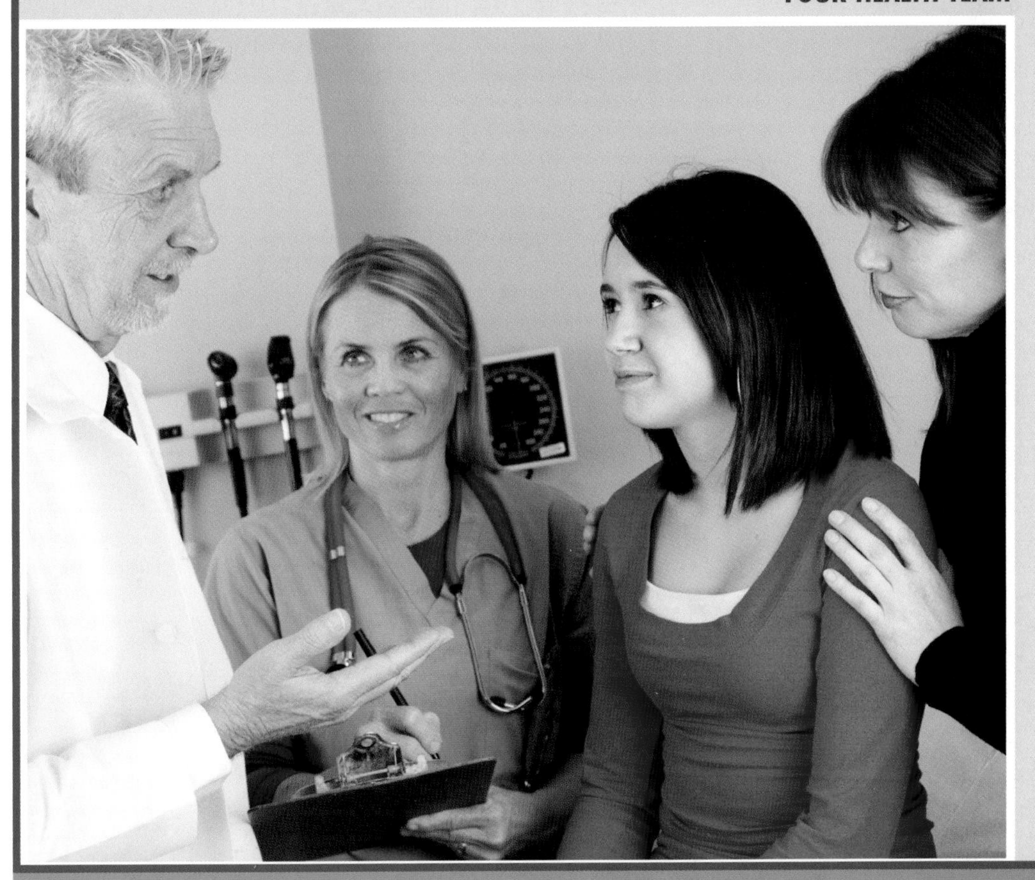

Don't hesitate to discuss with your health team members any concerns that you might have about PCOS or the medications they prescribe to treat the disorder.

experiences of others and share your own. There are also online organizations offering the latest information about medicines and therapies used in treatment programs. Several have discussion boards where teens can communicate with others who have similar conditions.

START A HEALTH JOURNAL

You might also start a "My Health" journal. This can be a notebook in which you simply record your feelings about dealing with PCOS. You can record

Keeping a journal can be a way of boosting your self-confidence about how you manage your health.

and track any symptoms that you might have experienced. Be sure to include a list of all your health care providers, how often you see them, what specific symptoms are being treated, blood tests, X-rays or other imaging studies, and any procedures that have been performed. List the prescriptions that you are taking, including any herbal or over-the-counter remedies.

During the next visit to your doctor, provide an update on how you have felt since your last appointment. Don't be shy about describing any new or unusual symptoms. This information provides the doctor with

Be sure to keep all appointments with your doctor and discuss any side effects that you may have when you are taking medications.

some clues about how you are responding to treatment. If you have been prescribed medicine, let your doctor know if it is helping to lessen any symptoms or if you've experienced any side effects from it. Never, ever stop taking medication that was prescribed for you without first discussing it with your doctor. Doing so can be dangerous. For people who discontinue their medicine to treat diabetes, high blood pressure, or a heart condition, this can be life threatening. Of course, if you experience a serious allergic reaction to a medication, such as hives, difficulty breathing, or swelling of your face or tongue, you should call 911 immediately. Furthermore, have someone call your doctor right away to discuss what happened so that you can be put on a different medication.

If your doctor didn't discuss a long-term treatment plan during your early visits, ask to work with him or her to create a plan for you. Discuss what role you can take in making your treatment happen, and don't be embarrassed to take notes in your health journal during your visit. Too often, people forget what was discussed after leaving a doctor's office. Your doctor may admire your determination to take control of your health. Be honest about sharing any feelings of anxiety that you may have. Your doctor should reassure you. Because knowledge can go a long way in creating confidence, ask the doctor to recommend articles or books about PCOS that might be suitable for you to read.

CHAPTER five

YOU HAVE PCOS, NOW WHAT DO YOU DO?

Are you a teen girl who has been diagnosed with PCOS? This is not the kind of news any girl wants to hear. Learning about this disorder and getting treated for its symptoms are really important. Treating it early on will help prevent or reduce PCOS-related complications.

What about now? What can you do about the signs and feelings that made you seek medical help in the first place? How are you going to cope with those symptoms? Consider this: you have been given a wake-up call at an early age. Tackling this condition can be tough, but there are many ways to manage and treat PCOS. You can choose to make the changes in your lifestyle—how you live your life—and can help control many of the symptoms that threaten your health. Start now!

SET YOUR GOALS

First on the list of goals for many, if not most, girls who have PCOS is to lose weight. According to the National Institutes of Health (NIH), up to 70 percent of all girls and women with PCOS are seriously overweight, enough to be considered obese. According to the government, obesity means that you are 20 percent over the normal weight for your age, sex, height, and build. Studies also show that PCOS is closely tied with obesity. Like many young people, girls with PCOS may gain weight during puberty, which helps them prepare for a growth spurt. For most teens, this fat begins to disappear after they have added inches in height. A girl who has a higher level of androgens because of a hormonal imbalance may retain weight.

Although indulging in that extra scoop of ice cream and not getting enough exercise might lead to weight gain, there are other reasons why people become obese. One NIH study suggests that many factors interact in complicated ways to cause people to become obese. People's genes, psychological makeup, behavior, culture or community, and the environment they live in may be responsible for their weight gain.

You may not be able to control some of these factors, but you can make the decision to change your behavior and become fit by creating a healthy lifestyle. Begin with how you eat, and take the steps recommended here.

Cut back on the amount of soda and high-sugar juice that you drink. Teenagers who drink lots of carbonated and caffeinated beverages eat more fast food. Avoid the "energy dense" foods, which contain more sugars and solid fats (pastries, fast food, or processed food). Eat more fruits and vegetables, whole grains, and lean proteins. Choose skim milk, yogurt, and other dairy products that are low fat or nonfat. Drink more water. This serves to keep your body hydrated and prevents you from feeling fatigued.

Always eat breakfast. You've heard that it is the most important meal of the day, and it is true. By not eating breakfast, you slow your metabolism, which can make you feel tired. When you're tired, you need to get some energy into your body. However, the worst way to get this energy is to grab a high-fat or high-sugar snack. Instead, you can start off the day with nutritious, easy-to-prepare foods, such as a whole-grain cereal and skim milk, a fruit and yogurt smoothie, whole-wheat toast with two tablespoons of peanut butter, or a protein bar and a banana.

How much sleep are you getting? A Harvard Medical School study on the sleep habits of teens shows that teens who sleep less than eight hours each night tend to have high-fat diets. This habit puts them at risk of becoming obese. Teens who are sleep-deprived tend to consume more calories from high-fat snacks than those who have at least eight hours of sleep every night. Why does this happen? Your lack of sleep can affect the hormones—leptin and ghrelin—that control your appetite. Altering how these appetite-controlling hormones function changes how and what you eat. Dr. Susan Redline, who conducted the Harvard study, noted that sleep-deprived teens have more opportunities to snack.

MOVE YOUR BODY

It is recommended that teens get at least thirty to sixty minutes of moderate exercise every day. Young children enjoy the energizing effects that running and physical play can offer, but teens often forget the health benefits and fun of physical activity or don't make time for such activity. KidsHealth.org reported that teenagers devote more than five hours to screen media—such as television, the Internet, and video games—every day.

Regular exercise can strengthen and protect your cardiovascular system (relating to the heart and blood vessels) from disease. If done on a regular basis, exercise can help you develop your large muscle groups and build strong bones. It stabilizes your blood sugar, which is particularly important for people who are at risk for type 2 diabetes, and it helps regulate your weight. Moreover, you gain self-confidence and self-esteem. Exercise can boost your energy!

Many teenage girls feel that getting exercise means that they'll have to join a health club. There are several other fun ways to work in at least an hour of exercise each day. Choose to be active by biking or walking to and from school instead of taking the bus or driving. Get a group of your friends to join you. Look into joining a girl's sports team, or take dance lessons. Even if you have two left feet, many dance programs welcome

Remember that being physically active can be fun. If you are not participating in school sports, organize an after-school exercise program with some friends so that you can improve the management of your PCOS symptoms and weight while having a good time.

beginners who want to improve their health. The form of activity you choose doesn't matter as long as you make an effort to spend less time watching television or surfing the Internet.

If you smoke cigarettes, stop. If you don't smoke, don't start. The same goes for drugs and alcohol. Smoking, drinking, and abusing drugs are choices that lead to bad habits and an unhealthy lifestyle.

Turning to friends and family members for encouragement during challenging moments can help you be proactive in dealing with your feelings about having PCOS.

GET SUPPORT

Be sure to keep appointments with your primary doctor and all other medical professionals who treat your symptoms. This is the only way that you can really monitor your health. At times, dealing with PCOS can be emotionally challenging. When you are feeling moody and need to talk about it, don't hesitate to turn to your health team—your parents, special friends, and perhaps members of a PCOS support group—who will help keep you positive. Writing in your journal about how you are feeling and the steps you are taking will give you the confidence to manage your PCOS symptoms and help you improve your health.

GLOSSARY

abstinence The act of voluntarily refraining from doing or having something, such as sex.

amenorrhea The absence of menstrual periods. Amenorrhea can be primary (which occurs in adolescent girls who haven't had their first period by the age of sixteen or so) or secondary (which occurs in women who have established periods but miss more than three or more periods in a row).

androgens A group of male sex hormones, such as testosterone, responsible for producing male sex characteristics.

contraceptive A form of birth control.

cyst A closed sac.

endocrine system The system of glands and cells that make hormones that are released directly into the blood and travel to tissues and organs throughout the body. This system controls growth, sexual development, sleep, hunger, and the way that the body uses food.

estrogen One of the female sex hormones produced mostly by the ovaries.

fallopian tubes Two tubes that allow mature eggs to travel from the ovaries to the uterus.

follicle A small structure in the ovaries that contains an egg as it matures.

genetics The study of heredity and the variation of inherited characteristics.

gland A group of cells that secretes hormones and other chemicals.

glucose Blood sugar that is used as a form of energy.

hirsutism An excessive growth of hair.

hormone A product secreted by living cells that circulates in body fluids (such as blood) to produce a specific function.

hypothalamus An area of the brain responsible for maintaining sleep, body temperature, hunger, and reproduction.

infertile Incapable of or unsuccessful in achieving pregnancy after a specified period of time, usually at least twelve months.

insulin A hormone produced by the pancreas that is essential for the metabolism of carbohydrates, lipids, and proteins and for regulating blood sugar levels.

menstrual cycle The complete cycle of physical changes a woman's body goes through (usually spanning twenty-eight days) to prepare the uterus for a possible pregnancy.

metabolism The chemical changes in living cells by which energy is provided for vital processes and activities in the body.

ovaries A pair of female reproductive organs located in the pelvis that produce eggs and female sex hormones.

ovulation The release of a mature egg from an ovary.

pituitary A gland at the base of the brain that produces hormones that regulate the menstrual cycle.

progesterone A female sex hormone produced by the ovaries after ovulation to prepare the uterus for pregnancy.

puberty The beginning of sexual maturity in girls and boys, usually beginning at age ten for girls and twelve for boys.

testosterone A male sex hormone that is produced by the testes, the male sex organs.

triglyceride A type of fat in the body and bloodstream.

type 2 diabetes A common form of diabetes related to insulin resistance.

uterus The pear-shaped reproductive organ that nurtures a developing baby until its birth.

FOR MORE INFORMATION

American Diabetes Association
Center for Information and Community Support
1701 North Beauregard Street
Alexandria, VA 22311
(800) DIABETES [342-2383]
Web site: http://www.diabetes.org
This association was created to inform the public about preventing, treating, and improving the lives of all people affected by diabetes.

Center for Young Women's Health
Children's Hospital Boston
333 Longwood Avenue, 5th Floor
Boston, MA 02115
(617) 355-2994
Web site: http://www.youngwomenshealth.org
The center's Web site provides teen girls and young women with carefully researched health information.

GirlsHealth.gov
8270 Willow Oaks Corporate Drive, Suite 301
Fairfax, VA 22031
Web site: http://www.girlshealth.gov
This organization's Web site is dedicated to promoting healthy, positive behaviors in girls between the ages of ten and sixteen.

Health Canada
Brooke Claxton Building, Room 1264D
Tunney's Pasture

Postal Locator: 0912D
Ottawa, ON K1A 0K9
Canada
(866) 225-0709
Web site: http://www.hc-sc.gc.ca
This is Canada's federal agency that helps people maintain and improve their health.

National Institutes of Health (NIH)
U.S. Department of Heath and Human Services
9000 Rockville Pike
Bethesda, MD 20892
(301) 496-4000
Web site: http://www.nih.gov
The NIH is one of the most important research centers in the world. It is made up of twenty-seven different institutes and centers.

National Women's Health Information Center
200 Independence Avenue SW
Washington, DC 20201
(800) 994-9662
Web site: http://www.4women.gov
This office provides information on women's health issues.

Polycystic Ovarian Syndrome Association, Inc.
PCOSupport
P.O. Box 3403
Englewood, CO 80155-3403

Web site: http://www.pcosupport.org
Volunteers of this organization respond to questions about PCOS by e-mail. The Web site has a teen message board for girls who are in high school and college.

Public Health Agency of Canada
30 Colonnade Road
A.L. 6501H
Ottawa, ON K1A 0K9
Canada
(866) 225-0709
Web site: http://www.canadian-health-network.ca
The role of the Public Health Agency of Canada is to promote health and prevent and control chronic diseases, such as cardiovascular disease and diabetes.

TeensHealth
Nemours Foundation
Web site: http://kidshealth.org/teen
The foundation's Web site gives information and advice about health, emotions, and life twenty-four hours a day so that teens can get the doctor-approved information needed to make educated decisions.

WEB SITES

Due to the changing nature of Internet links, Rosen Publishing has developed an online list of Web sites related to the subject of this book. This site is updated regularly. Please use this link to access the list:

http://www.rosenlinks.com/gh/pos

FOR FURTHER READING

Ashton, Jennifer. *The Body Scoop for Girls: A Straight-Talk Guide to a Healthy, Beautiful You*. New York, NY: Avery Trade, 2009.

Futterweit, Walter. *Understanding—and Reversing—Polycystic Ovary Syndrome*. New York, NY: Owl Books, 2006.

Gruenwald, Kate. *American Medical Association Girl's Guide to Becoming a Teen*. Hoboken, NJ: Jossey-Bass, 2006.

Harris, Collette, and Theresa Cheung. *The PCOS Protection Plan: How to Cut Your Increased Risk of Diabetes, Heart Disease, Obesity and High Blood Pressure*. Carlsbad, CA: Hay House, 2006.

Madaras, Lynda, and Area Madaras. *What's Happening to My Body? Book for Girls*. New York, NY: Newmarket Press, 2007.

Northrup, Christiane. *Women's Bodies, Women's Wisdom*. New York, NY: Bantam Books, 2006.

Orr, Tamra B. *Amenorrhea: Why Your Period Stops* (The Library of Sexual Health). New York, NY: Rosen Publishing, 2009.

Orr, Tamra B. *Ovarian Tumors and Cysts* (The Library of Sexual Health). New York, NY: Rosen Publishing, 2009.

Redd, Nancy Amanda. *Body Drama: Real Girls, Real Issues, Real Answers*. New York, NY: Gotham Books, 2007.

Rushton, Lynette. *The Endocrine System* (The Human Body: How It Works). New York, NY: Chelsea House Publishers, 2009.

Watson, Stephanie. *Endometriosis* (The Library of Sexual Health). New York, NY: Rosen Publishing, 2007.

Zied, Elisa. *Nutrition at Your Fingertips*. New York, NY: Alpha Books/Penguin USA, 2009.

INDEX

ABOUT THE AUTHOR

Before entering the publishing field, Frances E. Ruffin was a hospital lab technician. She has written health articles for magazines and is the author of more than forty books for young people. She lives in New York City.

PHOTO CREDITS

Cover, p. 1 © www.istockphoto.com/Diane Diederich; p. 5 © AP Images; pp. 7, 9 © Universal Images Group Limited/Alamy; pp. 11, 17 © Dr. Najeeb Layyous/Photo Researchers, Inc.; p. 15 © Custom Medical Stock Photo; p. 18 istockphoto/Thinkstock; p. 23 Reggie Casagrande/Photographer's Choice/Getty Images; p. 26 © Dr. P. Marazzi/Photo Researchers, Inc.; p. 28 Stephan Gladieu/Getty Images; p. 31 © www.istockphoto.com/Nicole S. Young; pp. 32, 39 Comstock/Thinkstock; p. 33 Tetra Images/Getty Images; p. 38 Tracy A. Woodward/The Washington Post via Getty Images.

Designer: Nicole Russo; Editor: Kathy Kuhtz Campbell;
Photo Researcher: Amy Feinberg